Simple Gifts
· A SHAKER HYMN ·

Chris Raschka

Henry Holt and Company

New York

Henry Holt and Company, Inc., *Publishers since 1866*, 115 West 18th Street, New York, New York 10011. Henry Holt is a registered trademark of Henry Holt and Company, Inc. Illustrations copyright © 1998 by Chris Raschka. All rights reserved. Published in Canada by Fitzhenry & Whiteside Ltd., 195 Allstate Parkway, Markham, Ontario L3R 4T8.

Library of Congress Cataloging-in-Publication Data / Simple Gifts: a Shaker hymn / illustrated by Chris Raschka. 1. Shakers—Hymns—Texts—Juvenile literature. 2. Hymns, English—United States—Texts—Juvenile literature. I. Raschka, Christopher. BV317.S56S56 1997 264' .23—dc21 97-16734

ISBN 0-8050-5143-0 / First Edition—1998
Hand-lettering by Chris Raschka. The artist used oil crayon on pastel paper to create the illustrations for this book. Printed in the United States of America on acid-free paper.∞

1 2 3 4 5 6 7 8 9 10

for Catherine, Kate, and Dan

'Tis the gift

to be simple,

'tis the gift

to be free,

'Tis the gift

to come down

where we ought

to be.

And when we

find ourselves

in the place

just right,

'Twill be

of love

in the valley

and delight.

When

simplicity

true

is gained,

To bow

and to bend

we shan't

be asham'd

will be

our delight

Till by turning,

turning

we come 'round

right.

About two hundred years ago, the religious people called Shakers began to live together on big farms. They thought of one another as brothers and sisters. So they shared everything. They made their own food, their own houses, their own tools, and their own furniture. What they built was simple and strong, elegant and useful. On Sundays and in the evenings, they sang and danced, turning and making big circles within circles, girls and women dancing in one direction, boys and men dancing in the other. One favorite song, "Simple Gifts," was probably written in 1848. It is still popular today, but it sounds different. Now it is often sung slowly. The Shakers enjoyed singing it rapidly to go with lively dancing. — C. R.

Simple Gifts

'Tis the gift to be sim-ple, 'tis the gift to be free, 'Tis the gift to come down where we ought to be. And when we find our-selves in the place just right, 'Twill be in the val-ley of love and de-light. When true sim-pli-ci-ty is gained, To bow and to bend we shan't be a-sham'd to turn, turn will be our de-light Till by turn-ing, turn-ing we come 'round right.